paper?

paper?

plastic?

plastic?

paper ?

plastic ?

?

plastic ?

plastic ?

paper ?

paper ?

paper?

paper ?

?

paper ?

paper ?

?

?

?

?

plastic ?

plastic ?

?

paper ?

plastic ?

paper?

paper ?

paper?

plastic ?

?

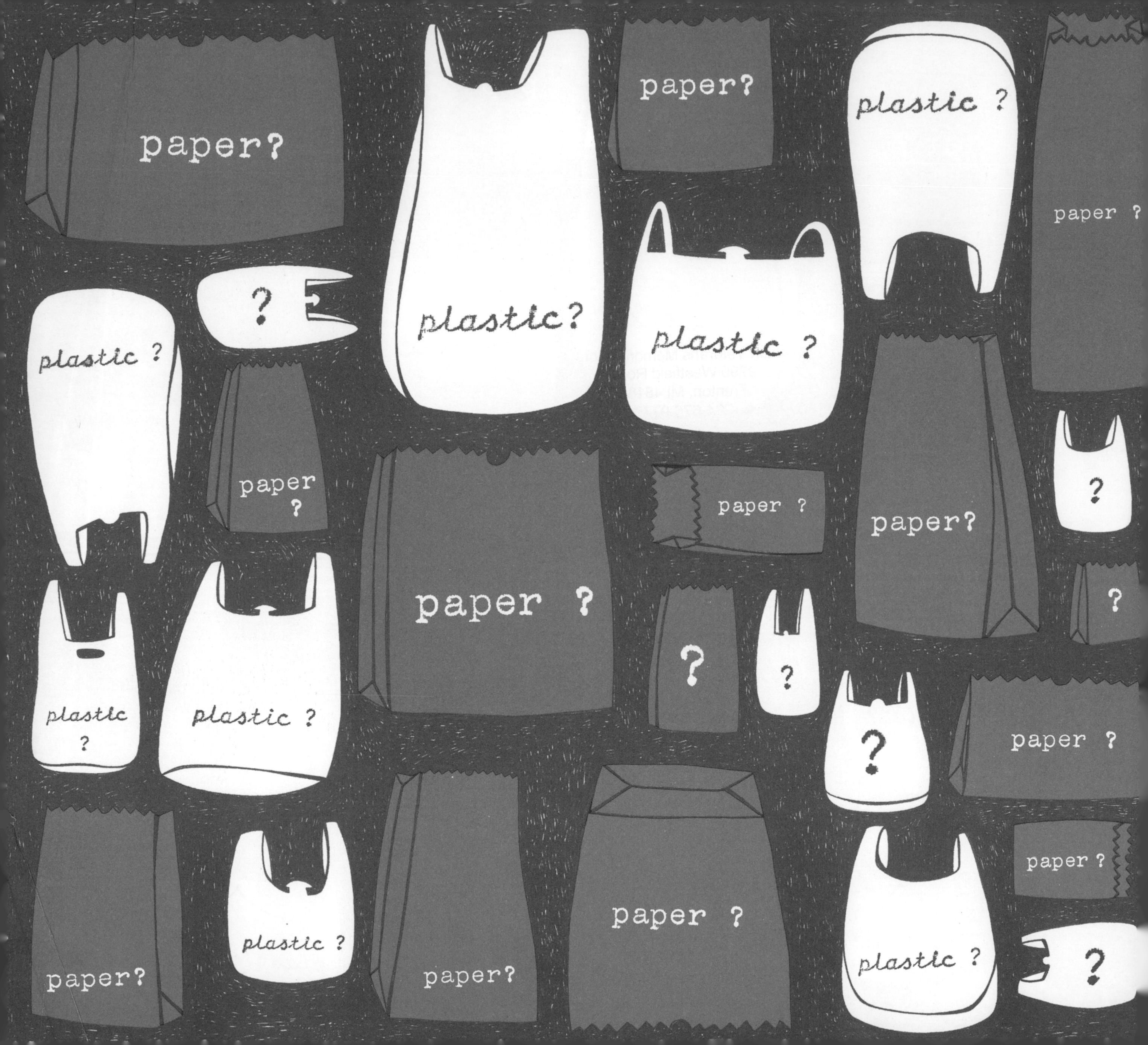

THE Runaway Shopping Cart

by
KATHY LONG

illustrated by
SUSAN ESTELLE
KWAS

DUTTON CHILDREN'S BOOKS

To Kaleb, my ray of sunshine

-K.L.

For my nephew Eli

-S.E.K.

DUTTON CHILDREN'S BOOKS A division of Penguin Young Readers Group
Published by the Penguin Group • Penguin Group (USA) Inc., 375 Hudson Street, New York, New York 10014, U.S.A. •
Penguin Group (Canada), 90 Eglinton Avenue East, Suite 700, Toronto, Ontario, Canada M4P 2Y3 (a division of Pearson Penguin
Canada Inc.) • Penguin Books Ltd, 80 Strand, London WC2R 0RL, England • Penguin Ireland, 25 St Stephen's Green, Dublin 2,
Ireland (a division of Penguin Books Ltd) • Penguin Group (Australia), 250 Camberwell Road, Camberwell, Victoria 3124,
Australia (a division of Pearson Australia Group Pty Ltd) • Penguin Books India Pvt Ltd, 11 Community Centre,
Panchsheel Park, New Delhi - 110 017, India • Penguin Group (NZ), Cnr Airborne and Rosedale Roads, Albany, Auckland 1310,
New Zealand (a division of Pearson New Zealand Ltd) • Penguin Books (South Africa) (Pty) Ltd,
24 Sturdee Avenue, Rosebank, Johannesburg 2196, South Africa •
Penguin Books Ltd, Registered Offices: 80 Strand, London WC2R 0RL, England

Text copyright © 2007 by Kathy Long
Illustrations copyright © 2007 by Susan Estelle Kwas

Library of Congress Cataloging-in-Publication Data

Long, Kathy.
The runaway shopping cart / by Kathy Long ; illustrated by Susan
Estelle Kwas.—1st ed.
p. cm.
Summary: When the shopping cart Kaleb is sitting in rolls out of
the parking lot and into the street, he has a wonderful time zipping
through town, chased by increasing numbers of characters in a
cumulative tale reminiscent of the Golden goose.
ISBN-13: 978-0-525-47187-5 (hardcover : alk. paper)
[1. Adventure and adventurers—Fiction. 2. Shopping carts—Fiction.
3. Humorous stories.] I. Kwas, Susan Estelle, ill. II. Title.
PZ7.L854Run 2007
[E]—dc22   2006010436

Published in the United States by Dutton Children's Books,
a division of Penguin Young Readers Group
345 Hudson Street, New York, New York 10014
www.penguin.com/youngreaders

Designed by Irene Vandervoort

Manufactured in China   First Edition

1 3 5 7 9 10 8 6 4 2

Kaleb and his mother were doing their grocery shopping, as they did every Friday.

Kaleb rode in the shopping cart, as he always did.

They bought milk, bread, eggs, cereal, juice, meat, and vegetables, as they always did.

They paid, as they always did.

The grocery boy bagged the groceries and took them to the car, as he always did.

But when they got to the car, something different happened.

Kaleb's mother said, "I forgot ice cream. I'll run in and get it. I'll be right back."

Just then the grocery boy's nose began to tickle and twitch. Then he sneezed—a great big sneeze. His head flew down. His hands flew up.

The cart began to roll.

It rolled across the parking lot and out to the street.
Kaleb waved as the cart picked up speed. As he was about
to hit a pole, he leaned to miss it and the cart turned.
The eggs flew out, but Kaleb stayed in.

Splat! Splat! The eggs hit the pavement.
Slippety-slide! The grocery boy hit the gooey eggs.

But the cart rolled on, into the street and down the hill, leaving the grocery boy behind.

Kaleb was laughing as he rolled past a little old man and a little old woman and their little old dog out in their yard. "Hi there!" he yelled, and waved.

The dog saw the shopping cart. She saw the grocery boy chasing the cart. It looked like such fun that she took off after them.

"Ruff!" said the dog.

"Fifi, wait!" the little old woman yelled.
Then she started chasing after Fifi,
who was chasing after the grocery boy,
who was chasing after the runaway shopping cart,
where Kaleb sat with his mother's groceries.

THE THIN MAN

The little old man looked up and saw his
wife take off after their dog.
"Mildred, whatever are you doing?" he yelled.

Then he dashed after his wife,
who was dashing after Fifi,
who was dashing after the grocery boy,
who was dashing after the runaway shopping cart,
where Kaleb sat with his mother's groceries.

A car came to a screeching stop as the shopping cart
zipped through a stop sign. The driver jumped out.
He shook his fist as the cart sped by.

Then he bolted after the old man,
who was bolting after the old woman,
who was bolting after Fifi,
who was bolting after the grocery boy,
who was bolting after the runaway shopping cart,
where Kaleb sat with his mother's groceries.

The cart rolled past the school, lickety-split!

"Hey, Nathan," Kaleb yelled to his big brother, who was outside at recess.

"Guys, it's my kid brother. We've got to save him. Let's go!" Nathan yelled.

So all the children zoomed after the driver,
who was zooming after the old man,
who was zooming after the old woman,
who was zooming after Fifi,
who was zooming after the grocery boy,
who was zooming after the runaway shopping cart,
where Kaleb sat with his mother's groceries.

The teacher was looking out the window and saw her class
chasing the runaway cart.
"Stop, class. Come back right now!" she yelled. But they kept
on running.

So she ran after them.
The principal looked out and
saw his teacher zipping after the class,
who was zipping after the driver,
who was zipping after the old man,
who was zipping after the old woman,
who was zipping after Fifi,
who was zipping after the grocery boy,
who was zipping after the runaway shopping cart,
where Kaleb sat with his mother's groceries.

The principal started to run, too.

Faster and faster the cart rolled.
Faster and faster everyone ran,
up and down hills, around and through
the streets until finally...

. . . the cart rolled into the parking lot, hit the curb with a thud, and stopped.
Then up came the principal,
    who was huffing behind the teacher,
    who was puffing behind the class,
    who was huffing behind the driver,
    who was puffing behind the old man,
    who was huffing behind the old woman,
    who was puffing behind Fifi,
    who was huffing behind the grocery boy,
    who had grabbed the runaway shopping cart,
    where Kaleb sat with his mother's groceries.

"It's the blue van over there," Kaleb's mother said to the grocery boy. Then she looked around.

"I didn't know Nathan's class was visiting the grocery
store today."
Then she looked at Kaleb.

He said, "Mom, we need more eggs."
Then he smiled.

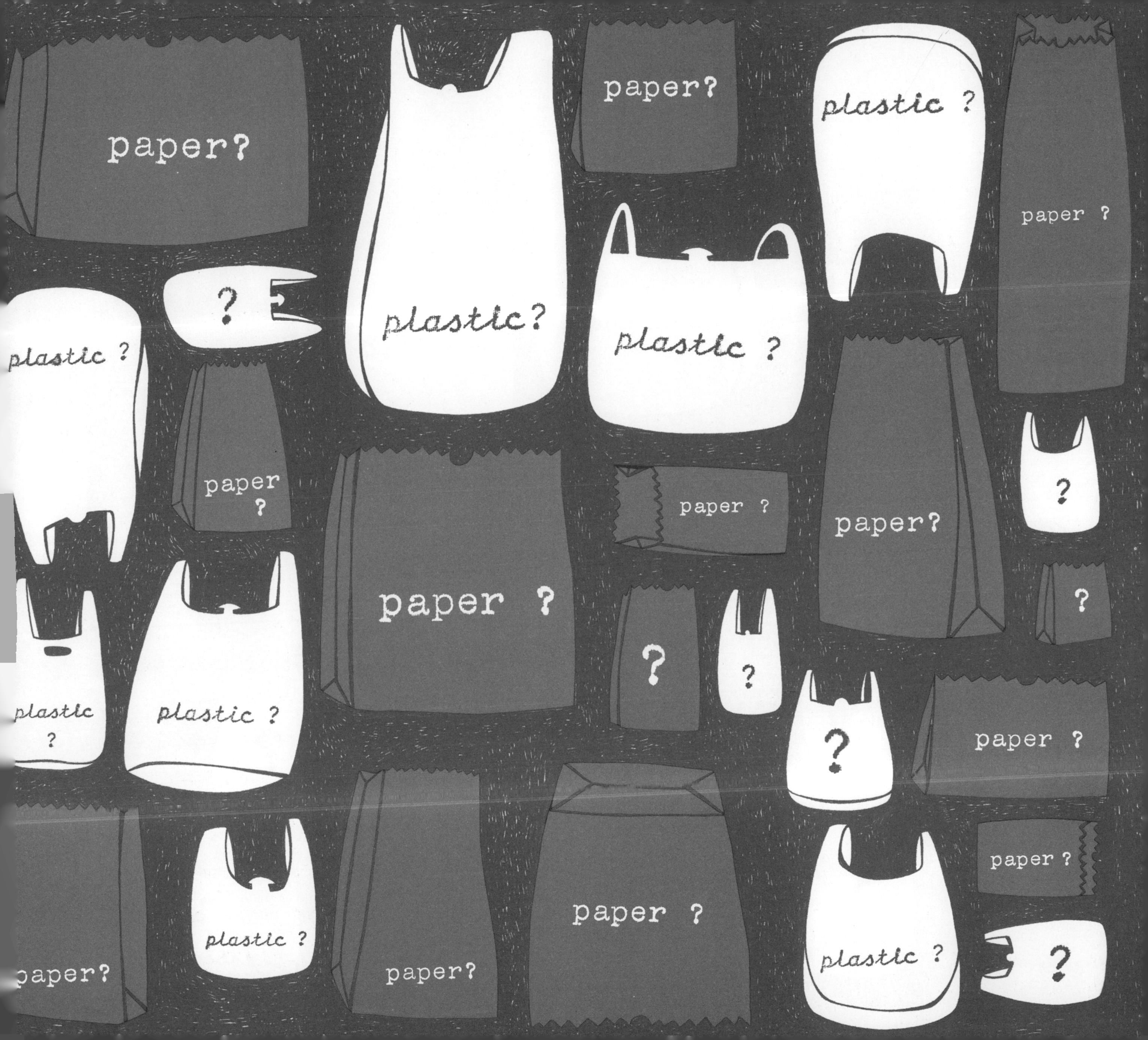

paper?

paper?

plastic ?

paper

plastic ?

?

plastic?

plastic ?

paper
?

paper ?

paper?

?

paper ?

paper ?

plastic
?

plastic ?

?
?

?

paper ?

paper ?

plastic ?

paper?

paper?

paper ?

plastic ?

?